MW01103542

Gundige oct '08 $15.85

Wolves

JoAnn Cleland

Bethany, Missouri

Photo Credits:
Cover © Photodisc; Title Page © Corel; Page 4 © Olga Mirenska, C. Paquin; Pages 5, 9, 11, 19 © Photodisc;
Pages 6, 17 © Corel; Page 7 © Marc Lamphear; Pages 8, 13 © Christopher O. Driscoll; Pages 14, 15, 18, 21 ©
National Park Service; Page 22 © IFAW/ International Fund for Animal Welfare/ S. Cook/ www.ifaw.org

Cataloging-in-Publication Data

Cleland, Joann
    Wolves / JoAnn V. Cleland. — 1st ed.
    p. cm. — (Animals in danger)

    Includes bibliographical references and index.
    Summary: Examines the physical characteristics,
behavior, and habitat of wolves, as well as why
they are endangered.
    ISBN-13: 978-1-4242-1393-1 (lib. bdg. : alk. paper)
    ISBN-10: 1-4242-1393-2 (lib. bdg. : alk. paper)
    ISBN-13: 978-1-4242-1483-9 (pbk. : alk. paper)
    ISBN-10: 1-4242-1483-1 (pbk. : alk. paper)

    1. Wolves—Juvenile literature. 2. Endangered
species—Juvenile literature. 3. Wildlife conservation
—Juvenile literature. [1. Wolves. 2. Endangered species.
3. Dog family (Mammals). 4. Rare animals. 5. Wildlife conservation.]
I. Cleland, Joann. II. Title. III. Series.
    QL737.C22C54 2007
    599.773—dc22

First edition
© 2007 Fitzgerald Books
802 N. 41st Street, P.O. Box 505
Bethany, MO 64424, U.S.A.
Printed in China
Library of Congress Control Number: 2006911295

Table of Contents

What Do Wolves Look Like?

Wolves are in the same animal family as dogs. Wolves look a little bit like dogs.

American Grey Wolf Golden Retriever Dog

Like a dog, a wolf has a pointed **snout**, a black-button nose and beady eyes. His ears stick up like little triangles.

What Do Wolves Eat?

Wolves eat meat. A wolf will eat any animal he can catch and can hold up to 20 pounds of food in his stomach.

How Do Wolves Hunt?

Wolves are good hunters because they can see, hear, and smell very well.

Sometimes a **lone** wolf will catch a small animal.

Most of the time, wolves hunt in groups. The wolf **pack** attacks a large animal from many sides.

They bite at the animal's legs and body.

Now that the animal is down, the wolves do not work as a team anymore. They fight each other for the meat.

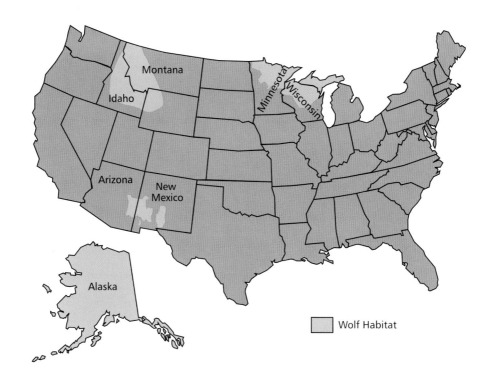

Montana

Idaho

Minnesota

Wisconsin

Arizona

New
Mexico

Alaska

Wolf Habitat

Why Are Wolves
in Danger?

Wolves live in the wild, but they are being chased out. People build houses where wolves used to run free.

People plant farms on big pieces of land. To save their sheep, cows, and horses, farmers kill the wolves.

People are killing rabbits, deer, and moose, too. Wolves have nothing to eat.

Will Wolves Become Extinct?

Once 500,000 wolves lived in the United States. Now there are only 9,000.

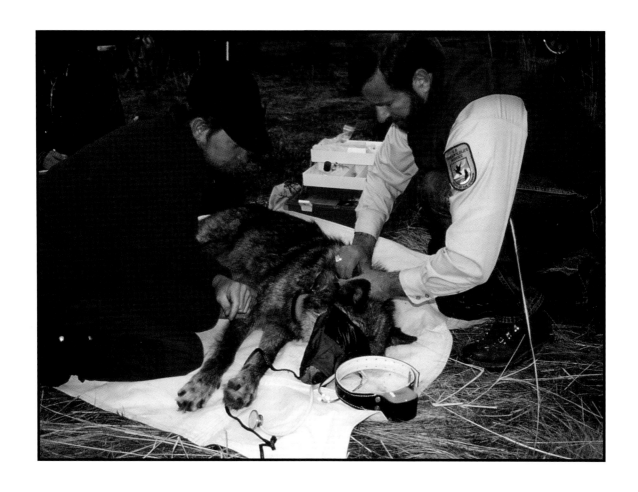

Some people are working to save them. In many places it is against the law to kill wolves.

Some people are taking wolves into big parks where they are safe.

Glossary

extinct (ek STINGKT) — gone from the Earth forever

lone (LOAN) — by itself or alone

pack (PAK) — group of animals that work and play together

snout (SNOUT) — long nose

Index

FURTHER READING

Dornhoffer, Mary. *Wolves.* Compass Point Books, 2004.
Markle, Sandra. *Wolves.* Carolrhoda Books, 2004.
Stone, Lynn. *Gray Wolves.* Lerner Publications, 2004.

WEBSITES TO VISIT

Because Internet links change so often, Fitzgerald Books has developed an online list of websites related to the subject of this book. This site is updated regularly. Please use this link to access the list: www.fitzgeraldbookslinks.com/ad/wol

ABOUT THE AUTHOR

Jo Cleland, Professor Emeritus of Reading Education, taught in public education and at the College of Education at Arizona State University West. Jo continues to work with children through her storytelling and workshops. She has presented to audiences of teachers across the nation and the world, bringing to all her favorite message: What we learn with delight, we never forget.